THE NIGERIAN

ERIC REESE

ISBN: 978-1-925988-28-4

"You gotta be able to smile through the bullshit."

- TUPAC SHAKUR

CONTENTS

Lago's streets were crowded which was typical for the morning rush hour as people were on their way to work and school. Traffic on the road was stalled and Debare Balogun was running late for his morning meeting.

He hurried through the crowds with his shining silver suit. Pushing through the marketplaces, Debare was determined to get there on time as it was a twenty-minute walk to his shop.

Inside Balogun Jewellery, his secretary, Daraja Agu, stood behind the desk welcoming him. She wore a ponytail and was dressed modestly.

"Good day, sir."

"Morning, Daraja."

"The gentlemen are waiting for you."

"Thank you."

Debare walked faster. If the clients didn't accept

his latest offer, it meant Balogun Jewellery wouldn't last much longer.

Debare's reputation wasn't the best in town. He was a scam artist and only few would work with him. Fixing his suit, he walked inside finding them seated at his roundtable.

"Morning, gentleman."

The men looked but didn't respond. Debare ignored them, setting down his suitcase.

"You're late."

"Traffic was bad."

"How's our project coming along?" asked Marcel, a Jew who was in Lagos trafficking diamonds and anything he could make money off of. He heard rumours of Debare's past business dealings but some-how, gave his support for this project.

"The gold transfer will begin in a few days, sir. We've made all the arrangements, so we just need your final deposit."

"We will not release the final deposit because our client has yet to receive the gold. Why is there a delay?"

"Uh, no sir, is there a problem?" Debare started sweating sensing he wasn't buying his story. Marcel whispered something to his partner in a suit beside him.

"The problem is you, Debare." Marcel picked up some papers he had on the table.

"Excuse me. Let me explain." Debare got up fixing his tie.

"You think you're fooling us, huh?" Marcel chuckled. "I know what you've been skimming money off the top. All the money; my men and I wasted on this damn project is in your bloody pockets." Marcel's fist banged on the table and its sound echoed throughout the office. Everyone heard him yelling including Darja.

"How dare you do this to your partner?" Marcel continued yelling.

Not only did Marcel and his men do the deal with Debare but Marcel rented him one of his shops to help Debare store the gold.

"Please forgive me, Marcel. Let me explain."

"If you don't get me my money by the end of the week, Kirikiri will be your new home. Do you fucking hear me?"

———

Marcel and the others left leaving Debare to sink in guilt. How would Debare find fifty grand in a week? *Only a miracle could save him.*

Debare packed his briefcase and left out for the

day. On his mind, as he walked through the streets; how he was going to repay Marcel.

The day went by, as Debare walked back and forth inside his flat. He lived in a place that only a government official could afford. Holding a half empty bottle of vodka, Debare was shaking.

"Why is this happening to me?"

He slammed the bottle against the wall and yelled, "Fuck!"

After hours of calling around to borrow money from those he knew, one colleague told him of a loan-shark named Shakale Oni in the red-light district.

"Shakale's usually at the Lexus Bar around 10 with his men. He won't be hard to spot; he wears an eye patch. Tell him I sent you."

———

The Lexus Bar was in the most dangerous neighbourhood in Lagos. It was an area known for prostitution, drugs, and robberies. The Nigerian was out of options, so he had no choice. He got dressed and lit up a cigarette. There were only a few street lights working as he walked in the night. People were looking at him weirdly as he passed by knowing he wasn't from the area.

As the Nigerian walked on, he got used to the staring. His focus was on finding the only person who might can help him; Shakale Oni. When Debare reached the Lexus, he ordered a drink.

For an hour, he waited for the man with the eyepatch to show up; drinking heavily. Debare was nervous and while he was on fifth, he saw a group of men entered, dressed in fancy suits. In the middle, stood Shakale with the leather eye patch. *Bingo!*

Debare watched as they made their way to a table. Debare put his glass down and walked over. "Shakale Oni?" The Nigerian acted as if he knew the man. Shakale looked up, agitated.

"What do the fuck do you want, man? I have no time for your kind tonight."

"I need to have a word with you. It's important."

"Not in the mood today." He waved Debare off with his hand.

Debare stood, not moving. "I am in need of something from you, sir and I'm not a beggar. I'm a businessman."

Shakale looked at Debare and the Nigerian's heart was racing. He has never been in such a desperate situation.

"Speak."

"I desire Naira from you. My friend, Oluwa told me to see you."

Shakale's men looked serious as they waited for

their boss to respond. Shakale shook his head and then smiled.

"Why did you say that from the very beginning? Sit down." Shakale pointed to a chair beside him. "How much?" asked Shakale taking a sip of Scotch while his men looked on.

"Fifty grand in US dollars."

Shakale turned to his men. His entourage dared not look back. Shakale turn back to the Nigerian and replied, "You see my men. They would never ask of me of such amount and you, a stranger has. What do you need it for, anyway?" Shakale started to believe the Nigerian was sent by the police.

"I'm in a major debt, sir. I own a jewellery shop in town and if I don't pay that amount, I'll have to close it down by month's end or sooner."

Shakale nodded, uncertain if he should give Debare the money. Yet, Debare resembled someone from the upper class.

"Who sent you again?"

"Oluwa."

"That's my man. Give me a day and you'll have it." Sipping on his Scotch, Shakale turned his attention back to the night scene. Debare exhaled thanking him.

"Matter of fact, come here first thing in the morning. Consider this your lucky day."

"Thank you, sir. Thank you."

Debare tripped over something as he got up.

Now that the Nigerian had Shakale's backing, he wanted to call Marcel. Shakale offered him a drink, but Debare declined, excusing himself to the restroom. He locked himself inside the last stall, dialling Marcel's number.

After a few rings, Marcel picked up. "What do you want!?" His voice echoed through the bathroom.

Debare cleared his throat. "I'll have your money."

Marcel paused and then chuckled. "Who did you scam this time to get my fifty grand?"

"Friday morning, I'll be at your office." Debare banged, not wanting to hear another word.

No one was in the restroom when Debare turned on the sink and splashed water on his face. He tried forgetting where he was at. It was dark and red inside with paper towels all over the floor. The Nigerian understood Shakale was more dangerous than Marcel. If he didn't return the money, Shakale would get him first.

Debare gripped the sides of the sink as the running water continued running down his face.

"Fifty grand is a lot of money--" a man said, startling Debare. The Nigerian looked in the mirror and saw a white man dressed in black standing a few feet away.

"Excuse me?"

"That's a lot of money. Am I right?"

Debare turned around. "Why were you eavesdropping on my conversation?"

"I wasn't really. I was taking a shit in this dump and overheard your boss who seems angry, huh?"

"What is it to you?"

"I know a lot of what goes on around here." The man began walking to the bathroom's exit.

Debare tried passing him but the man pushed him back.

"Well, I mean I work for people that know a lot of things that are happening around here." The man took out a gun from his back.

"Who the fuck are you? What the hell do you want?"

"Call me your fucking knight in shining armour."

"What? I have no business with you."

"I work for MI6 and I'm here to take your ass with me."

"Over my dead body."

Debare pushed him and the man pushed back, putting Debare in a chokehold. Debare tried fighting back as his eyes began rolling in the back of his head. "Let me go!" he pleaded and the man eventually did so. The Nigerian was on the ground gasping for air.

"What do you want? I have no money," said the Nigerian struggling to catch his breath. The man kneeled beside him and pointed his gun to Debare's head, "I can turn you in and you'll rot in Kirikiri until you fucking die."

"Please don't."

"Get up, you piece of shit!"

With his hands on the back of his head, Debare got up sweating.

"Now, do as I say. No questions or else." The man grabbed his phone and dialled. "Unless you want to walk out here naked, it's your fucking choice."

Debare didn't say anything further. As they were exiting, Debare looked around to see if Shakale was still around, but it appeared that he left. Once outside, a black van screeched pulling up to and the white man pushed Debare inside.

"Listen, I borrowed money from one of the most dangerous men in Nigeria at that bar. At least, let me take care of my problem."

"I'll fix your problems. Just enjoy the ride. We have a long flight ahead of us."

CHAPTER 2

"Welcome, to the United Kingdom." A service agent welcomed everyone who departed the plane.

Just a day ago, Debare was almost ready to pay off Marcel and now he's thousands of miles away. His fate was either spend the rest of his life in Kirikiri or die at the hands of Shakale and Marcel. Why am I in England? he wondered. Debare was given an address and told to say nothing.

The flight was nine hours, and Debare couldn't sleep. It was the first time in years since he boarded an airplane. He dragged his suitcase through airport customs and then on towards the exit.

A cab driver waiting for his next fare spotted Debare. "Hey, my friend. Get inside."

Debare gave the address to the driver and while on the road, he didn't speak.

The fog and cloudy skies of London surprised Debare. He snapped a few photos with a new phone given to him. It had only a few apps and one contact in case of an emergency. "We're minutes away."

"Thank you, sir." Debare nodded, saying nothing else. The Nigerian was eager to see what he got himself into.

Five minutes later, the driver said, "We're here."

Debare paid and got out. The building in front was huge and constructed futuristically. He went to the gate and found it locked. There was an intercom on the side. He pushed the button and an old woman answered.

"Military Intelligence 6, how may I help you?"

"My name's Debare Balogun from Nigeria. I was told to report here by one of your agents."

"Your name again is?"

"Debare Balogun."

The gate buzzed. There was a long driveway leading up to the main entrance. Unmarked black and white cars were parked on both sides of the driveway.

Debare entered and saw people in suits engaged in what appeared to be operations. The receptionist stared at him and figured he was lost.

"May I help you?"

Debare turned as if he didn't hear her. "Oh, oh. "I

was told to come inside, and I'm clueless about where to begin."

"You're Debare Balogun. Am I correct?" She asked looking at her computer.

"That would be me." Debare nodded while scratching the back of his head.

"The general is expecting you on Level 5, Office 230." The lady smiled and handed him a visitor's pass to access the elevator.

The elevator was crowded, and no one went to the fifth floor except Debare. He got off and walked down a dark empty hallway to Office 230. There were voices talking when Debare knocked.

Then there was a silence before someone yelled, "Come in."

Debare walked in, seeing men and women dressed in military fatigue. They appeared to be the high-ranking police but none were wearing badges or name tags.

"Good day, gentleman."

"And who you might be?" an old man yelled from afar. Debare turned and saw him sitting and thought he was in charge.

"Debare Balogun, sir." Debare straighten himself as if he was ready to salute.

Everyone turned their attention to the Nigerian.

Debare waited for the old man to respond but was kept in suspense because he didn't quickly.

"Well, we've been expecting you. Ladies and Gentlemen, please if you have work to do, take it to your areas."

A few got up and left while some others took seats at a round table in the room's center.

"I am General Robert Wilson. Have a seat, Mr Balogun. Did I pronounce your name correctly."

"Yes, you did, sir."

Debare tried sitting at the farthest place from the General, almost tripping over some cables. The general stood up, opened a drawer and took out some files.

"Why am I here, sir, if you don't mind me asking?"

"Why are you here? This lad is funny." The group of agents laughed and General Wilson chuckled.

"With your history of fraud, we thought you'd be the perfect candidate for this operation," Robert walked over to the table and handed some files to Debare. "Let's just say I have chosen you for something very important that requires your expertise."

Debare looked over the papers seeing that were numerous charts and stats he couldn't understand. "What are these, sir?"

"Russia's making a lot of money. They have the strongest economy in Europe and Asia."

Debare crossed his arms.

"I'll say this again, Russia has the highest GDP today," said Robert, having second thoughts. Debare was more focused on the papers then what the General had to say.

"There's no coincidence that their GDP has skyrocketed. Thieves like yourself use Russia's black market all the time. Am I correct?"

"Maybe."

"Don't fucking maybe me, Debare. I know you fucking criminals like the back of my hand. Fucking diamonds in Nigeria are replicas for these Russians. That's why Marcel Verhoeff wants his money back. There's no collusion, I guess."

Everyone laughed.

"Tell me. Are you up for a mission, son?"

"It depends."

"It depends on your life. You are trying to say?"

Debare was puzzled.

General Wilson continued, "Last week, Russia was all over the fake news because two Cullinan diamonds were located at the Popigai Crater".

As General spoke, Debare wondered how It was even possible. There were only less than ten found in the world.

We estimate "One Cullinan diamond's worth to be around two billion dollars."

The amount took aback Debare. The others listened while typing on their laptops.

"Debare, we need you to go to Russia as a refugee and see what's going on. We need to know the truth about whether these diamonds are in good hands or bad pockets."

Debare's heart raced as he learned about what his role would be. If he refused, he would eat bean soup in Kirikiri for life or killed.

"Sir, I'm not so—"

"Well, you have no other choice. I'm not asking."

The other agents stared at Debare as if they were ordered to imprison him if he didn't follow along. The Nigherian nodded slowly and one agent signalled for Debare to follow.

"You will be changing identities for the mission and your past will be forever lost," explained Robert as Debare was getting up.

"Our agent, Brian will give you all the details, so don't let us down, Debare. This is what we Brits call "life or death." Debare noticed the white man from the club, waiting at the door.

———

The Nigerian was no longer in charge of his destiny. This mission had no guarantees. What would happen to his business in Lagos? Marcel and Shakale? His secretary Daraja? Debare had so many twists and very little answers.

His stay in the United Kingdom was brief. Ever since he was a boy, he always wanted to visit London. Now when he had the chance, it was under duress. This was no vacation. His life was hanging in balance by MI6. Debare left the building with Brian after getting briefed for hours. The Nigerian was in a black van on his way to Heathrow Airport. Brian gave him an extra suitcase telling him not to open it until he landed in Moscow. He was also told there was one satellite phone inside. MI6 instructed not to make any calls unless ordered.

Debare wasn't close to his family but asked Brian to allow him to leave them a message just in case something happened. The order was granted, so he texted his mother:

"I miss you terribly, Mama. I'm away on business. I hope my absence doesn't worry you. Mama! You'll hear from me soon. Love, Debare."

His greed for money made him grow apart from his family. They couldn't have their own being a fraudster. They knew Debare's transactions were dishonest, but still, they called begging him for money when they were in trouble.

Made to believed the Nigerian was headed to the

airport, the driver diverted off to a secret military aircraft hanger. From there, Debare boarded a plane along with a few other men. The estimated flight time to Moscow was three hours and thirty-five minutes. Everyone was told not to speak.

There were strong patches of turbulence throughout the flight. The small plane rocked back and forth for hours scaring everyone. When it finally landed, there were cheers and whistling. Debare got off with two suitcases and observed they were at a makeshift airstrip. The snow was falling heavily, and he was confused about where to go next. One man nudged him and pointed at a truck ahead. The passengers hurried inside, and in the heavy snow, the truck didn't leave any traces.

———

While moving, Debare received a text stating, "St. Hemmingway 13, a group of refugees are gathered, ready to speak to the Minister. Be there."

The instructions were confusing. The passengers were silent as the truck arrived in Moscow within the hour. Debare was dropped off across the street from the UK consulate. The snow was lighter in Moscow. A man met him outside and took one of his suitcases. Debare didn't ask questions watching the man go back inside. The Nigerian started his phone's GPS to find St. Hemmingway 13.

It was a fifteen-minute walk and Debare was out of breath as he walked through the snow. The combination of jetlag and little exercise didn't help. He didn't know where he'd lodge but knew he had to hurry. When Debare arrived, there was a group of Africans in front of a building, protesting. He was at the right place and joined the crowd, pushing his way through to almost the front. 'The Federal Assembly' was engraved in the building's front.

A small batch of Russians walked out and stood at the podium minutes later. One man began speaking in broken English.

"Today is a day of celebration, I'm here to say I stand with you!" The man raised his fist. Everyone in the crowd cheered. "I am deeply saddened by the fact you are forced to flee your countries' violence and poverty and now you are being exploited to greater harm; trafficking, prostitution, and persecution. I'm here to say as long as I'm a part of this Parliament, you're welcomed to our country!"

As the demonstration went on, Debare lost focus until his phone texted: "These are the profiles of the people standing on the platform."

Dabare skimmed through them quickly, seeing they were all part of the Parliament. Debare assumed

MI6 was there with him. As long as drones exist, the man is always looking in. A man next to the speaker caught the Nigerian's attention. He appeared to be in charge of Russia's high-end nightclubs according to his profile. How does this man have time to run them while working in Parliament?

His phone buzzed again. "Follow Boris Petrov once the speech is over."

Debare waited patiently. T-shirts, food, and water were handed out from volunteers. Why are they giving out T-shirts in minus-5 temperatures? Debare's phone buzzed again. "Put the tracker inside his suitcase."

The crowd began clearing out, and Debare saw Boris leaving alongside with his bodyguards and the other Parliament members. He took out the tracker from his bag and held it tightly. As he was catching up to Boris, he played out what he wanted to do in his head.

"Sir Petrov!"

Boris turned around with his men.

"Something fell out of your suitcase!"

"What may it be?" he asked as Debare came closer. One of Boris' bodyguards tried blocking his way.

Boris appeared annoyed. "This is your pen." Boris took it from Debare placing it in his suitcase. "Your work in helping us refugees is highly appreciated. Thank you, sir." Boris shook the Nigerian's hand and then proceeded with his entourage to an unmarked car.

The sunshine came out as Debare walked through the streets in the direction of the UK consulate. When the Nigerian reached, he received a call from an unknown number, telling him the next steps of his mission.

Debare's station was already set up allowing him to tap into Boris Petkov's tracker and listen when he arrived home. Boris' conversations were boring as the interpreter's voice made the Nigeria fall asleep at times. All he talked about was the hot chicks he had, the whisky he drank and an upcoming meeting with Putin he was looking forward to. Roughly into the second hour, Debare was interrupted by a phone call from an unknown number again.

"Hello?"

Then there was a long pause.

"You shouldn't have shown your face, Debare."

It was Brian. The Nigerian rolled his eyes as he looked inside the fridge seeing it was full.

"Well, how was I supposed to get to him without the fucker seeing me?"

"Don't give me that shit, you dumb fuck."

"Give me an order that's clear or I'll do it how I like."

"Do you want to go home to Kirikiri? Watch your mouth." Brian hanged up.

"Doko mi," shouted Debare in Yoruba which means "suck my dick."

Just when Debare was about to throw the phone against the wall, the sound of a phone rang on the feed streaming Boris. Debare pressed the button on his laptop to read the English interpretation.

"Where are the diamonds? I need my money right away," pleaded Boris.

A man on the line was calculating prices. "They've already sold two, sir, and the cash was deposited."

The call ended, and Boris went to the bathroom to take a shit. Debare stopped the feed. Other two, huh? That meant the Russians dug up four at the Popigai Crater instead of two. He rushed to call Brian back and he took a long time to answer.

"I've got news for you. The diamonds are four not two, sir."

"What? But there were only two according to our intel? Then, the other two will--."

Brian appeared to be proud of the Nigerian now. "Hmm. Listen, tonight you'll need to sneak inside the

Ministry of Finance building. There's one man named Aleksandar Andreev. Get inside his office and gather whatever Intel you can. I will send you a file briefing you on what we are looking for specifically." Debare listened while biting down his nails.

"Yes, sir," replied Debare and then he hung up. Debare rolled the recording, again and again, looking for anything else until he became sleepy. Tonight, Mr Balogun will start his first true mission.

* * *

Two hours had passed and Debare was ready. He walked out on the streets, dressed in an ushanka (fur hat) and black fur coat. It was cold as hell as he approached the Metro station. It will be his first time taking the train. Back in Lagos, no one who had money had patience to be cramped up with hundreds on Nigeria's daily commute. Some even hired helicopters to escape the dreaded traffic.

At 10 PM, the train was packed; each passenger was pushing one another trying to get a seat. Debare sat and wondered what nightlife they had if they were working so much on the weekdays.

After a few stations, he got off at Kursky Station. The Nigerian lit up a cigarette and strolled toward the Ministry of Finance in the Siberian cold. Once the Nigerian spotted the monumental building, he plotted how he would sneak inside. There were two guards out front, holding AK 47s. Debare stood farther resembling a homeless man looking for a place to stay.

He encircled the building to the back entrance. It was locked with a security camera moving overhead. Brian texted him, "I will take care of the cameras and door."

Seconds later, the cameras shut off, and the door beeped. The halls inside were dark and the Nigerian put on his night-vision glasses. He took a right to the stairs leading to the top floor. Debare's footsteps were flat matching a professional burglar.

When Debare turned up a hallway, he bumped into the night janitor. The Nigerian's heart raced as he was dumbfounded.

"Hey, what are you doing here?" the man said in Russian.

Debare grabbed the old man, choking him to sleep. He then hit him on the back of the head with his gun's butt to finish the job. Debare dragged him to the nearest maintenance closet and put him inside.

"Get to Aleksandar's office without fucking getting caught," whispered Brian in Debare's earpiece.

"Yes, sir."

The last floor was where the Minister's office was located. Brian didn't have Intel on a specific room number and Debare knew he had to get there some-time tonight. After passing a few offices, the Nigerian focused his attention on the last door down the hall which appeared newly constructed. He scanned the name on the door with his phone, and the phone's translation came up with Aleksandar's name. Debare turned the knob, but it was locked. Looking behind, he opened his sac and grabbed two metal pins. After a few seconds, the Nigerian got the door open and felt proud; reflecting his scamming for years had finally paid off.

He shut the door and searched Aleksandar's drawers for anything tied to the Diamonds. There were Playboy magazines and other documents but nothing. He put his hands on his head and blurted "Odi Oshi" which means "stupid fuck." Moments later, the Nigerian accidentally knocked over a lamp. Someone rushed down the hall and Debare hid in a closet. Aleksandar's door opened slightly and a security guard peeped inside with his flashlight.

"Is anyone in here?" the guard said in Russian. He came closer to the closet but didn't open it. He then circled the room, finding the broken lamp on the ground. "Let maintenance handle this shit. Damn, rats again!" The guard closed the door.

Debare waited for a bit before coming out. He was determined to find the files. On the other side of the room, was a safe with a keypad."They have to be inside."

Debare kneeled taking out talc powder from his sac and spread it lightly around the keypad and brushed upwards, leaving little traces along the buttons. After two failed attempts, the safe was cracked. There were rubles, sex toys, and folders inside. His eyes grew when he saw the bills. There had to be thousands of rubles. "Don't touch the money. I know you," alerted Brian from the earpiece.

The Nigerian took snapshots of the files, checking them although they were in Russian. The last one caught his eye. There was an invoice from yesterday in the range of 4 billion dollars. Taking a clear photo, Debare sent it to Brian. Perhaps it was the money from the two missing Cullinan?

The Nigerian's phone buzzed right away and it was Brian. "Track the individuals involved in the transactions and take any evidence back with you." Debare instantly felt like a real spy.

He placed a mini-recorder underneath the desk, grabbed some folders and left. Creeping down the halls, Debare made it out undetected. When he got home, Boris was chatting on his live feed.

"This activist is in on the fraud as well," mumbled Debare.

Another text message from Brian came in. "Meet

me at City Space in thirty minutes. Don't be late." Debare changed, came back out and entered the location on the app. "It's cold as a motherfucker out here," said Debare lighting up a cigarette as he closed the door behind.

    * * *

City Space is one of the most popular bars in Moscow at the city's tallest building known as the Vostok Towers. Debare arrived early, waiting for Brian at a table near the back. People were dancing, drinking and having a good time as Moscow never sleeps. Debare ordered a Scotch and watched crowds of beautiful women resembling supermodels jam the dancefloor. A few minutes later, Brian showed up.

"You did well." Brian admitted not looking at Debare while calling over a waiter.

"Finally, Brian."

"Who told you, you can call me by my first name?"

"Myself," Debare said sipping on his drink.

"Enough of this blabbering and let's get down to work. Here, take this."

Brian handed Debare a folder with a picture of a middle-aged woman clipped on the front. The name 'Alina Grekova' was written in black underneath it. Debare glanced inside as the waiter came back with Brian's drink.

"I'm ready."

"The woman in the picture is the Minister of Education." Brian sipped while flipping the folder's pages for Debare. "And here are some of her felonious activities."

The words 'Drug trafficking, prostitution, human trafficking' caught Debare's eye.

"How did she become the Minister of Education?"

Brian sidestepped Debare's question. "Alina's a brunette with bangs that hang low over her forehead. They say her grandmother dropped her when she was a baby. The bangs cover the large gash. She's originally from Poland but moved here with her daughter. Some say her daughter's a drug addict, and that's the reason they came to Moscow."

Brian took a long sip and then finished:

"The point being Alina Grekova is involved in all types of shit. Believe me! Tomorrow, the Parliament will hold their final session before taking a break for the holidays. I'm positive she'll be there. Follow her after the session closes and find out who she'll be meeting with. Familiarise yourself with her past and get some rest".

Brian got up and strolled out, leaving Debare to pay the tab. "Omo Ale (Bastard)," shouted Debare.

Debare went home a few hours later and tried digging up anything he could on Alina Grekova. There wasn't much online except for a few articles on how well she's done with the kindergartens. There was also an article of her posing with some local high-school students at a hockey game. Debare closed his laptop and went to bed.

CHAPTER 4

"It's too early in the morning for this shit," conceived the Nigerian as he reached the Metro station. The journey was thirty minutes long and there weren't any empty seats. Debare held on and after a few stops, he decided to get off to grab some coffee. He didn't realise it would be a twenty-five-minute walk to the Kremlin Senate from his location. After arriving, he stood by a bench near the front entrance and took snapshots. Minutes later, a few unmarked government cars arrived in and a few senior officials got out, embracing one another. Debare spotted Alina Grekova in the last one, greeting her colleagues. She hugged them and then they proceeded inside. Alina was dressed up as if she was attending a holiday party.

"Something big is going on."

Her driver walked away and went to take a break

with the others. They chatted and smoked not far from their vehicles. Debare crept up to Alina's, took some snapshots and placed a tracker underneath. Once he came up, a man startled him. "What are you doing here?"

"I don't know Russian, sir. I'm a tourist and I love this car," said Debare staring at the others all wearing black suits with matching black shoes.

"I've always wanted to buy a car like this. Do you know who's the owner?"

The driver shook his head trying to make out Debare's accent. Moments later, he responded.

"I do. She's the Minister of Education. By the way, man, I like your country America. You have the fucking hottest chicks."

"Thank you." Debare chuckled.

The driver looked over at his colleagues who were now looking and suddenly changed facial expressions.

"I must ask you to leave right away."

"Okay, man. You got a cool car here! Remember to come see us in America. You'll get a hot chick."

The driver saluted and the Nigerian walked off.

Debare received a text from Brian stating the meeting was in progress and to wait around until it concluded. The Nigerian smoked a few cigarettes while strolling through the area. An hour later, Brian texted him, "There's a motorcycle parked behind the

Senate for you. License plate number: H647xCC-77. Its keys are in the left jacket."

————

Ninety minutes passed and Debare received a text stating the Ministers were coming out exchanging their goodbyes. Alina proceed to get in the car with an unknown man. The Nigerian put on his helmet and followed. Keeping his distance, they drove through downtown Moscow; passing by many high-end restaurants and strip clubs. Alina's car finally stopped at Turandot. Debare took snapshots as Alina kissed this unknown man in public.

"That guy must be her lover."

The two lovebirds walked inside and Debare parked across the street. The Nigerian then proceeded to the restaurant's front and was stopped. "Do you have a reservation, sir?" the clerk said in broken English.

"No, I do not but I need to get in. It's cold and I have a friend coming."

"I am sorry sir but that's not possible. You'll need a reservation and can come in when your friend arrives."

The clock resumed his work when Debare pulled out a hundred-dollar bill and placed it on top of the desk.

"I'm sure you can find an empty table and a glass of

wine for a dear friend?"

"Let me escort you right in. Come right this way, sir. Hurry, it's cold out."

Debare followed and the restaurant was nearly empty.

"Here you are. Your drink will be up shortly."

Debare looked over the menu, seated not far away from Alina. A waiter came over a few moments later asking for his order.

"The cheapest thing," said Debare swatting the waiter away. Alina's lover pulled out a huge ring and placed it on her finger. Her face lit up as she repeatedly kissed him. Debare took a few snapshots and waited calmly for his order.

A text came on his screen: "Hack Alina's phone. I just upload a virus to yours. Open the NFC and get close."

Minutes later, Alina got up and went to the restroom. The Nigerian got up at the same time and went over to her table and sat.

"That's a lovely suit, sir. Where did you get it from?" Debare said staring at Alina's handbag.

"Excuse me, who are you? You're in my lady's seat." The man spoke in broken English.

"I work for the VIP," pointed Debare to his right, intentionally flipping over the handbag. Alina's phone fell out and Debare reached for it.

"So sorry, sir. I'll pick up everything."

Debare stooped and put his phone on top of Alina's. The program took a few seconds to start, and it began counting by percentages. "Uploading 35%."

"What the hell are you doing?" the man said standing up.

"The makeup spilled all over, sir. She has a lot of beauty products."

"Now at 50%," read the screen. Debare pulled the table cloth causing the wine to stain the man's pants. The man ran away to the restroom to get the stain off. Debare's phone now was reading, "80%." Debare heard the sound of Alina's high heels approaching.

"95%."

"Oh shit!" gasped Debare.

Alina arrived. "What's going on here? Why are my things on the floor?" she said in Russian.

"100%."

Debare stood up handing Alina her handbag and straightened himself up. "Sorry lady, I don't speak Russian. You have some fine beauty products. Take care and have a pleasant evening."

"Thank you, sir." Alina was astonished not knowing what happened.

Debare left a one-hundred-dollar bill for the man to clean his suit and then rode off.

"It's done." Debare texted Brian.

"Good, now you can check her phone history and eavesdrop on her lovely chats."

"Alina's in love."

"With whom?"

"I think it's with a minister. He wasn't there at the refugee rally. I don't know who he is."

"Find out."

Brian hung up the phone down and yelled, "Fuck."

———

Back home, Debare began tracking Alina while having Boris and Aleksandar on the split-screen monitor. With the help of the MI6, he wrote every number that appeared on Alina's phone. There was a person named Andrei Trubanov, the acting Minister of Finance who frequently called. He was present at the refugee rally. Debare glimpsed through her photo gallery looking for more evidence on her activities. He found many photos of her daughter and family. However, there was one that showed a large diamond resembling one of the Cullinans.

"Alina's in on the heist. Are the entire cabinet colluding as well?"

For hours, he replayed Boris's tracker for more details. In his notes, Debare wrote: "It appears the last diamond was last supervised by Boris. One diamond was sold so far, and the statesmen divided the profits. Alina was the first to receive a payment according to the invoice found in Aleksandar's office. Aleksandar was paid, but it doesn't mention when. He also has strong ties with Alina in a few businesses. There are five more suspects to investigate." Debare marked the remaining seven ministers at the rally that day for further probes and sent his report to Brian.

Around 9 AM the next morning, the Nigerian's phone had awakened him. It was Brian. "I got you in one of the parliament meetings as a security guard, be there in 30. Your uniform's in janitor closet A." Debare jumped out of bed and showered.

The Nigerian made it to the Senate building in 20. It was cold outside and only a few dared to come out to smoke. Debare entered the back entrance through the garage and had trouble finding the janitor's closet. After circling around the building, he found it and shut himself inside. He found the security uniform folded on a chair and an earpiece. The Nigerian quickly got dressed, fixing his hat and placed a small camera on his collar. "This shirt looks good." Debare still didn't know what room the meeting was being held in.

"Hey! Buddy," yelled Debare, approaching a fat security guard at the end of the hall. "Do you speak English?"

"Yes."

"Where's the meeting? They have me stationed nearby just in case, someone spills their drink."

"Haha, in Hall Room—. Wait, a minute. I haven't seen you before. Have I?" The guard hobbled towards Debare.

"Yeah, I've been around. Just been sick lately, but this is my first day back."

The guard paused. "Hmm, you're Peter from Sudan?"

"Yes, sir."

"Now I remember. Vladislav told me about you the other day, you can go. It's right down in Hall Room B."

"I never heard of anyone named Peter from Africa," whispered Debare to himself.

As Debare drew closer, he spotted Alina talking to Boris outside the door. Debare lowered his head and passed by. A dozen government officials were seated. Alina laughed as she entered inside with Boris. Once they sat, the two kept chatting until the meeting started. Debare heard the sound check in his earpiece for the language interpretation.

———

The clock in the room read ten, and the ministers' meeting is now in session. As others came in almost late, two security guards had closed the doors and instructed Debare and his co-guard to keep quiet. An older man was seated at the head of the table started speaking. "Ladies," he said pointing at Alina and "Gentlemen," while smiling at the rest. "As you may know, Russia is now the leading economic powerhouse in all of Europe and Asia. All thanks to our friend, Boris."

The speaker started clapping and the others followed along. "Let's say, Vlad had a major role in transferring the diamonds."

Who's Vlad? There was no intel on that name.

The speaker continued, "Vlad will come back home from his trip shortly."

"I think we should throw him a party," shouted one minister. Everyone cheered, but Alina and Boris stayed silent looking agitated.

"Anyway, let's get to work, shall we? With our growing economy, many companies from abroad want to invest in our country nowadays. We have to take advantage of the momentum. You, the ministers, will be in charge of the areas of our incoming investments." Everyone present gave him their undivided attention.

Meanwhile, Debare observed Alina and Boris' body language keeping his head down, so they wouldn't recognise him.

The speaker went on to continue. "Collectively,

twenty of the world's biggest companies want to invest in our country so there will be fifty thousand jobs which would make our economy even stronger. We'd like a twenty-year commitment from each, guaranteeing that they'll not take our money and just run." Everyone clapped except for Alina and Boris.

"Shouldn't we first offer small contracts for 2 to 3 years to see how they do?" interrupted Alina raising her hand.

"We are in no position to negotiate at this time. It's either take-it-or-leave-it."

"I mean twenty foreign corporations seems like a stretch operating at one time in our country without adequate oversight. They'll have enormous revenue being that Russia's taxes are currently the lowest in 25 years."

"Alina, look at the bright side, over fifty thousand Russian citizens will have good-paying jobs. We wouldn't have to worry about them going abroad supporting other nations' economies," stated the head minister while flipping through papers. "And we will have first-hand knowledge about the interests of these corporations before they're made public."

The speaker had a history of out-talking Alina which caused her to keep quiet as another minister stood up. "With the growing economy and these latest developments, I think we need to raise the workers' salary to about fifteen percent for the forthcoming year."

Debare recognised him from the rally. It was the Minister of Finance, Aleksandar Andreev.

Most approved the notion and clapped. Alina rose shouting, "Absolutely not! This will bring down our country in less than six months."

"Alina, calm down 15 percent isn't that much. I think we can handle it with the new investors coming in. A happy country is a safe one. No one will question what is being done behind the scenes as long as they are happy."

"This is crazy. The economic forecast of adding fifteen percent will raise our budget so quickly that it will crash our stock markets to the ground. There will be a recession and businesses would pack up and leave Russia. I see we're not on the same page here, Minister," said Boris sharply.

The president of the Parliament interjected and said, "I am in support of this motion, and I'll leave it for you all to vote on it in our next assembly after the break."

Alina grabbed her purse and left out in a rage, leaving the door open. She rushed pass Debare, not recognising him. After she left, the session recommenced, and there were a few more things on the table. A few more disputes took place between Boris and the rest of the council. By the end, everyone seemed frustrated with one another and was ready to go on break.

Debare's headed for the front gate. The same security spotted Debare passing through again and stopped him. "Excuse me, sir. Who are you again?" Alongside him was a man of African descent dressed in the same uniform.

"I'm Peter, sir."

"But, Peter's right here with me. You're an imposter. Come with me right away." The supervisor ordered Peter to stand put while he dealt with the Nigerian.

As they were heading to his office, Debare told him to look down because the old man dropped something.

The guard looked and Debare tripped him. The Nigerian ran as fast as he could to the exit passing by the African and out the door. The real Peter stood there laughing.

"Stop him. Stop him. You dumb fool!"

Peter raised his arms as the old man ran past him into an elderly woman who just entered.

"Hello, my son. I need directions," asked the old woman.

Out of respect, the old man stopped and answered giving Debare more than enough time to escape.

CHAPTER 5

"I can't believe you did that! Are you out of your fucking mind?" yelled Brian inside Debare's flat.

The Nigerian was drunk; replaying in his cognizance what happened earlier. He wasn't in the mood for Brian's schoolboy lectures.

The Senate Building breach was the top story of the hour. Luckily, Debare's face wasn't identifiable, but footage showed a black male running out. Brian knew this may compromise the mission, and if it were up to him, he would have pulled Debare out at once.

"What do you have to say for yourself?" Brian hit the table earning very little attention from Debare.

"I made a mistake, don't we all?"

"You cannot afford to make mistakes as a spy. I told you not to get caught, but you did the exact opposite."

Debare sighed. "The old man caught me leaving. Your Intel sucks. I was supposed to be in the clear."

"You are on a mission and trained to avoid detection."

"What's my next mission then? I'll do a better job next time."

"Oh! Your next mission? Don't even fucking bother." Brian spat toward Debare. "Robert assigned another agent, so MI6 won't be needing you any longer."

"Oh my god! I'm ruined. I deserve a second chance. I don't want to Kirikiri."

Brian didn't say anything right away. He sat down on the couch and watched more of the news coverage while having himself a drink. Debare in the meantime vomited. Brian carried him to the bathroom and leaned him over the toilet.

Brian cared about his agents and didn't accept any mistakes. Mistakes mean dead lives. He accepted that he might have picked the wrong person. Debare came out, barely able to walk and sat down next to Brian.

"Sober up, I've got a quick assignment for you."

The Nigerian looked pitiful and Brian felt a bit remorseful on how he spoke to Debare.

"Listen up! Alina Grekova's daughter, Gala is hosting a party at the Night Flight; a popular club here.

All you will need is VIP access." Brian scrolled through his phone, searching for something.

"How will I get in?"

"I'll take care of it but you must look presentable." Brian looked at him from his head to his toe. "Pick out the best you have. I'll have your access in a few hours."

"And Debare, don't fuck this up."

———

Midnight came, and it was time for Debare to leave. He rode his bike downtown and within minutes, found the club. Crowds were in line, waiting to go inside. Debare walked up to the bouncers and they looked skeptically at him but when the Nigerian flashed his VIP ticket, they made room for him to go inside.

He ignored the stares of the Russian chaps and sat down near the bar. Techno music was playing and everyone on the dance floor was jumping up and down.

"What would you like to order, sir?"

"A beer.".

While the Nigerian waited, he examined Gala's picture on his phone. How was he going to approach her without looking like a creep? The Nigerian looked older than most of those partying.

"Here you are, sir."

Moments later, Debare spotted Gala. Her beauty

was stunning. Then, she disappeared into the crowd. The Nigerian looked up to see if she was on the second floor. She wasn't there but popped up dancing with the crowd on the first. Debare took a sip of his beer not pulling his eyes away from her.

"Do you need anything else?" interrupted the bartender.

"No, thanks," Debare smirked, turning his attention back to Gala. He wondered if Gala knew her mother was deceiving the citizens as being the Minister of Education.

Minutes later, she approached the bar, leaning close to Debare. He smelled her heavy perfume. "A Tequila, please."

Debare watched her chuck it down. Her friends ran over and cheered, yelling her name. This scene reminded him when he was hanging out all over Lagos. Drinking friendships don't last forever, and Debare forgot most of his friends once he started his business.

"Hey, bartender. Do you speak English?"

"Yes, I studied it in school."

"Who is that girl over there?"

"Oh! Believe me, you don't want her," said the bartender while serving other patrons.

"I wonder why?"

"She's the bratty Minister's daughter. She only hangs out with rich boys."

"So that means I have no chance?"

"Probably not. She's in a league by herself."

Debare was instructed to tail her, and not to do anything crazy. This mission was quite boring but it was Debare's chance to redeem himself. Meantime, Gala started dancing with two guys who were grinding against her. Her skimpy outfit looked like it cost a fortune. The young girl kept coming to the bar every few minutes ordering more drinks. The Nigerian took more snapshots of her dancing erotically and looking at her wasn't a waste of time.

Another woman who was more beautiful than Gala came in. She almost pushed Debare off the stool to sit down. She danced and moved provocatively as waited for her drink. Her body was mesmerising and Debare kept looking at her ass. Whoever she was, she could have been a fashion model. Minutes later, she accidentally tripped over the big stool in front of her, spilling her drink on Dabare. The Nigerian was grateful he was wearing black.

"Oh my God, I'm so sorry!" The woman grabbed a napkin from the counter dabbing it on Debare's shirt.

Debare grabbed the napkin from her hand and tried doing it himself. The woman apologised over and over, but Debare kept saying it was okay.

"I don't even know what I was looking at."

Debare looked at her and then to her bosoms,

seeing a rather odd rock resembling a diamond; lying perfectly in the center. It looked like the Cullinan but no one could tell.

"Come with me over to my table, I'll make it up for you." The lady smiled and it left Debare puzzled.

Debare didn't want to miss out the opportunity. The woman grabbed the Nigerian by the hand and pulled him through the center towards the elite VIP section. At her table, were two other men about her age who looked like they were her bodyguards.

"What's your name?" the woman hummed in the Nigerian's ear, licking her lips.

"Peter."

"I'm Nikita."

"Nice to meet you, Nikita." The men at the table didn't introduce themselves and stared at Debare. "This is Evgeni, and that's Nikolai." Again, none of them greeted.

"Good evening, gentlemen."

"Okay, well do you want something to drink?"

"I think I've had enough for tonight." Debare looked away trying to spot Gala, but she wasn't around.

"What's wrong, baby?"

"Nothing. About that drink you offered, I've changed my mind." Nikita handed him a glass of vodka.

"Cheers!"

Nikita watched Debare chuck it down in one shot. "Why are you here alone, baby?" Nikita whispered over the loud music.

"My friends, they left earlier," said Debare looking at her bosoms. It was one of the Cullinans but how so?

"Well, I'm not letting you leave soon, now that your friends are gone." Her hands rubbed down his chest, making little gestures with her fingers. The Nigerian wanted to laugh. He never met a woman like this, driven with such tenacity yet classy. Her movements were alluring. The Nigerian watched her seductively moving her ass as she called him over to the dance floor, wiggling her finger. Debare looked seeing everyone dancing except for her two bodyguards. Nikita quickly wrapped her arms around the Nigerian and he could feel her warm breath on his neck. He then wrapped his arms around her waist, still trying to locate Gala to no avail.

"Sorry about Nikolai and Evgeni. They're not very nice to strangers."

"It's fine, I'm still here because of you." The Nigerian kept looking at her bosoms.

The song changed to an upbeat track, and Nikita let Debare go. She went over to Nikolai and Evgeni, forcing them to dance with her. Debare sat, sipping on his drink watching the action for a few minutes.

"I'm going to the bathroom, sweetheart." Debare felt Nikita's hand on his head. He put his drink down smiling, looking at her ass as she was walking away.

"I'll be back and you don't go nowhere," Nikita yelled before disappearing. Her bodyguards, Nikolai and Evgeni then walked up to Debare angrily.

"What's your business with Nikita!?" said Nikolai.

"Excuse me?"

"You heard my friend, what do you want from Nikita?" demanded Evgeni. The Nigerian kept his composure.

"Nothing, she invited me over to pay me back for ruining my shirt."

"You have jokes, huh?"

Evgeni balled his fists, but Nikolai grabbed him. "Stay away from her," said Evgeni, but Debare just shrugged.

"Tell Nikita that. I'm only here for tonight."

The two picked up their things from the table and appeared to be leaving. Debare didn't give them no attention and continued sipping his drink. Moments later, Nikita rejoined the Nigerian and took a seat. "Where are Nikolai and Evgeni?"

"They left early, I guess and didn't want to say goodbye."

Nikita rolled her eyes. "I didn't like them anyway. My father sent them to protect me," explained Nikita roaming through her bag. "I'm not feeling well, Peter." Her eyes started closing as if she was about to faint.

"What's wrong?"

"I think I might have been poisoned," slurred Nikita.

The men responsible for protecting her were trying to kill her. It was almost three in the morning. The night club was packed, and it looked like the party wasn't anywhere close to ending. When Debare got up to help, gunshots were heard from the front entrance. Everybody screamed, and the music was still playing. Nikita came back to her senses.

"Nikita! We know you're in here. Just give up!" A man screamed loudly.

"We don't want that pretty little face of yours to get hurt now, do we!?" Another man yelled in Russian.

Debare carried Nikita and tried his best not to get caught under the flashing lights.

"There she is! Get her!" Debare thrust Nikita to run. People were yelling and they ran by and headed towards the back. When they made it outside, Nikita said, "There's my car, the keys are inside." She pointed at an expensive black Mercedes at the end of the parking lot.

"Stop right there!" Debare looked back.

A gunman pointed at Nikita and was about to pull the trigger. Debare saw he couldn't help, so he jumped in front of her. The gunman fired and the bullet struck Debare's leg.

"Oh, God! It hurts."

Nikita drew her gun out and shot the man in the head. "Fucking bitch," yelled Nikita as she knelt to assist Debare.

She shouldered him inside the car and drove to the nearest hospital as Debare was losing lots of blood. Nikita pulled Debare out and shouldered him towards the reception.

"Help me, please! This man has been shot."

Others sitting down, who were more worried than Nikita, got up out of their seats to give Debare a place. His blood was splattered on the white hospital floors from the entrance to the seating area.

"What happened!?" A doctor came running up, inspecting Debare.

"Someone shot him in the leg! He's losing blood!"

"Nurse, prepare the operating room. This one can't wait."

"Yes, Doctor. Right away."

Two nurses shouldered Debare and the doctor told Nikita to wait in the lobby. She put her hands on her head and was visibly shaken. An old woman came from behind and comforted her telling Nikita everything will be okay.

CHAPTER 6

Nikita waited in front of Debare's hospital room; waiting for the doctors to give her permission to go inside. Last evening, they removed the bullet from his leg, which just missed breaking his tibia. The Nigerian's pain was so unbearable that the doctors told her to come back in the morning.

She left but returned, being the first visitor to arrive at the hospital in the morning.

"You can go in now." A nurse told her.

Nikita walked in closing the door finding Debare awake.

"Hey!" said Debare seeing her enter. He tried sitting up but struggled and Nikita ran over to help.

"How are you feeling, baby?" Nikita kissed Debare on the lips.

"Better, the meds they gave me knocked me out," smiled Debare looking down at his leg.

"You'll feel the pain when it wears off." Nikita smiled sitting down on a chair nearby.

"I guess I'll enjoy it, while it lasts."

"So who were those men after you last night, Nikita?"

"I don't know."

"You're not telling me the truth."

Nikita got up, turning her back. "Know your place, Peter."

"My life is now in danger, and I deserve to know what the fuck is going on."

"Those men were after something." Nikita turned back around. "It was a big mistake. I had something that should have stayed locked away."

"What was it, Nikita?" Debare acted as if he didn't already know.

She looked at him stupidly.

"Don't act like you didn't see it on my neck. You were looking at my breasts and ass all last evening."

"I think you're right about that," laughed Debare.

"The diamond. You stupid freak!"

"Is it real?"

"Of course, it is. It's one of the most prized diamonds on Earth. I know you heard of the Cullinan. Haven't you?"

"Oh shit!"

"I can't say anything else." Nikita walked over to the window, looking at the street. "They will come after me again." She turned back around to face Debare. "And I don't know when."

"So, what are you going to do?"

"I'll have to go into hiding."

Nikita was too young to defend herself. Debare could offer for her to stay at his place, but he was on a mission. He needed to find out where she got that diamond from and how deep her ties are with the Parliament.

"Frankly, I'm here to make you an offer." Her tone turned serious wasting no time. "I want you to be my personal bodyguard, Peter."

"Nikita, I'm not fit for the job."

Nikita came to his bedside and rubbed his face.

"Few would ever take a bullet for me, and you don't even know me." She said rubbing his chest with her tender white hands.

"Hire someone that's Russian."

"I trusted no one in my life until the other night." She started opening his shirt and moving her hands downwards.

"I will pay you a lot of money." Her head lowered to his cock, which was now bared.

"I-- I'm yours, under one condition," Debare

repeated as Nikita sucked and licked. "That I don't get killed."

"Believe me, our safety is my only priority, baby," whispered Nikita as she was enjoying pleasing the Nigerian. He leaned back and enjoyed Nikita snatching his soul.

———

Debare was discharged from the hospital after a week. Brian had secretly come by to see how Debare was doing. He debriefed Debare's story, telling him to rest, and focus on getting closer to Nikita. Brian didn't tell Debare he had someone else working on the mission; a British operative, Vlad who was half-Russian and British. He's been working with the Parliament for years as a government contractor in the oil sector. Vlad had very strong ties to the ministers and their families.

A taxi was called to pick up the Nigerian and take him to Nikita's. The fading sun's rays burned his skin when he got to the front entrance of the hospital. The Nigerian put on his sunglasses and limped to the taxi. The driver immediately took his bags and placed in the trunk.

As they drove through Moscow's neighbourhoods, Debare looked over his new messages. There was one from an unknown number that read, "I expect you -

Nikita." He smiled, knowing big brother was still watching him.

Twenty minutes later, the taxi halted at Nikita's. Debare was ready to pay but the driver told Debare it was covered. As the Nigerian got out of the car with the help of the driver, he checked out the surroundings. There were mansions with large gardens and the streets were clean. Debare put his bag and Brian texted him.

"Don't forget to turn on your phone's interpreter." The Nigerian rang the bell twice before Nikita answered through the intercom. Debare heard people laughing in the background.

"Good morning, mon amour?"

"Morning! It's Debare."

"Come in!" The gate then buzzed open.

There were colourful flowers on each side and the walkway's tiles were fancy. Loud music was coming from inside the house and there were guests walking around with drinks. As Debare made his way in, Nikita came out with two men looking stunning.

"Peter!" yelled Nikita holding a bottle of champagne. The men were looking strangely as the Nigerian approached.

"What's going on here?"

"Oh, I must've forgotten to tell you!" She said

placing the champagne on the table and embraced Debare. "I'm hosting tryouts today!"

"What kind of tryouts?"

"Oh, you'll see, mon amour. For now, drink some of this champagne with us. We are celebrating life!"

"I'm good."

Nikita went back inside where her guests were chatting and laughing at something one gentleman had said. Debare watched as they poured themselves drinks laughing and almost drunk. Nikita was pleased. Moments later, three young ladies had entered the garden, outfitted revealing tops. Debare put his hand over his mouth, wondering what is really going on.

"Your names and ages, please," Nikita spoke in English as she made sat.

"My name is Tanya, and I'm 21 years old." She was a tall slim girl with black hair. The young woman nodded looking at the next.

"I'm Sonya, I turned 24 yesterday." The young woman tucked a strand of hair behind her ear and smiled, placing her hands on her hips.

"Calina, I'm 23 years old." The last woman was so bashful that it made Nikita grin.

"Okay, girls tell me a little more." Nikita kept asking them questions and jotting down their answers.

At first, Debare thought Nikita was running a modelling agency. But was proven wrong when Nikita ordered the girls to remove their clothes. He sat entertained and didn't say a thing.

The girls were then ordered to play with themselves and had ten minutes to climax. Each was given toys and everyone in the room enjoyed their moans. Then, they were escorted to a room to get dressed. Nikita paid them and then went to the bathroom while telling everyone to take a break.

"Excuse me, by the way, what the hell does Nikita?" asked Debare standing next to two men smoking cigars.

One responded, "I guess she hasn't told you yet, huh?"

"I guess not."

Both men laughed and Debare tried but couldn't. The second man tried to cut him off his comrade from speaking but couldn't. "Our boss runs the largest prostitution ring in Russia. There will always be ladies around to fuck as long as you are employed."

Both men laughed loudly holding their hands over their mouths to suppress the noise. Debare realized he had been duped into working in the black market.

"It's weird she hasn't told you yet. I mean you're working for her after all. Am I correct?" said the second man in sunglasses while sipping and looking at the girls' CVs.

"Yeah, man. I knew that, but I was responsible for her gold deliveries and got transferred here today."

"Cool. Well, it's nice meeting you. What's your name?"

"Peter." Debare shook hands with the gentlemen and excused himself. Two minutes later, Nikita came back and Debare didn't wait for her to continue. He pulled her to the side and grabbed her firmly, "Are you running a prostitution ring?"

"Is there something wrong with that, mon amour?" Nikita freed herself from the Nigerian's grip.

"Yes, a lot."

"Listen, Peter. I don't have time for this right now. I'm working."

"I don't either, so be honest with me, why did you hire me?" Debare's voice grew louder.

"Because I felt sorry for you. Now, please don't make a scene in front of our special guests."

"I've been honest with you and almost got fucking killed. Now, you're the one deceiving me."

"Look, if you want to go, then go. Don't think I can't find a replacement for you."

"Fine, I'll stay. But don't get us killed with your foolishness?"

As Nikita was leaving, she grabbed the Nigerian by his cock in front of the guests and said, "I told you in the beginning, your job is to keep me safe. I'll deal with this black thing later this evening."

Debare went to the side, hiding his erection but checking out the remaining women who came for the next hour. After the girls and men walked out, Debare saw the couch was so wet that Nikita would have to throw it away. Nikita closed the front door, and came back to Debare, kissing him on the neck. Debare tried resisting and Nikita went down to her knees, opening the Nigerian's zipper.

Twenty minutes later, Nikita finished with Debare and left Debare in the room. The Nigerian assumed he could leave. As he was heading to the front gate, Nikita's guardsmen pointed their weapons at him and instructed him to go to the back. A guard pulled out a room key and handed it to the Nigerian. The Nigerian then saw Nikita come back and out.

"You will stay with me for at least half of the month and I'll be back this evening for more." Nikita went into the kitchen with two of her maids.

"Oh my God!" Debare groaned as the guards escorted him to his quarters.

Two weeks later and after loads of sex with Nikita, Debare finally got back home, seeing much hadn't changed. He thought Brian would have come by to clean it up, but there was no sign of anyone entering. Brian didn't even bother calling him after he left the hospital. Debare could not wait to talk to Brian which was quite strange.

The Nigerian threw his duffle bag on the couch and sat wondering what was going on back in Lagos with his shop and secretary. Brian told him he'd take care of it but he still felt sorry for Daraja.

He turned on the TV finding most of the channels in Russian. "Are there any fucking Africans on TV here?" sounded Debare. The BBC was the closest thing to Nigeria that he could find, so he turned up the volume.

"A foreign spy is being sought by Cheka, and we have leads in the case," said the Minister of Finance." Debare turned it off. "No more going out. I'm a wanted man. Shit, where the hell is Brian? " Debare dialled Brian's number and after ten rings he answered.

"Hello, Brian. What's up? The police are still on me. Get me the hell out of here."

"I told you before that's not my problem, I can't do anything about it, now."

"Muthafucker," muttered Debare.

"What did you say?"

"Man, they will kill me once they discover me. Abort this mission or whatever words you guys use."

Debare walked over to the balcony and looked outside to see if anyone was there.

"They don't have your ugly face, so they won't discover you. There are many refugees in the country that look just like you. All the black guys look the same, right?"

"You fucking cunt!"

"Cheer up dude and hey man, it's good you called after drowning in all that Russian pussy. Shit, look at it like you were on vacation.

"Yeah, right."

"Anyway, I need you to assist Austin tonight."

"Who's Austin?" My replacement?"

"Yes, and you need to be a lookout for him tonight. He has an important mission objective. Please don't get fucking caught."

Debare rolled his eyes. "Alright fine, where?"

"The Ball at Winter Palace. The ministers will be there and while they're smooching, Austin will go in and question Vlad. We got everything set up. All you have to do is stand by the door. It's a piece of cake."

"There's nothing easy working with you, guys. Anyway, isn't Vlad working for us?"

"Yes, but this guy is different. By the way, they sure look like fucking brothers. Anyway, Vlad is the one who found the Cullinans and is probably the middle man for the transactions. Your tape from the Senate

Building connects him but we still need more proof. Remember the Ball, 9 PM and don't be late."

———

Fifteen minutes before nine, Debare got dressed for the Ball. As he was leaving, he received a message: "Meet me at the back gate.—A.A." which stood for Agent Austin.

Debare giggled at his strange signature and locked his door. Believing his motorcycle was outside, he realised that he left it at the club. "Shit, I need to call a taxi."

Ten minutes late, Debare reached the Ball and went to the back entrance, noticing dozens of expensive cars parked. He lit up a cigarette, expecting Austin to show up on time but he didn't. Minutes later, a black van pulled up in front of the Nigerian and a white man hopped out. "Debare Balogun."

"Yes."

Austin buttoned up his suit jacket while offering his hand.

"Austin?"

"Right, your job is simple. Just do as I say. Understood?" Austin's cockiness annoyed Debare.

"Alright."

"We'll be waiters for tonight."

"Waiters? Brian told me--"

"Mission objectives have been refreshed."

"God damn! You guys work on the fly?"

"We don't. It's just part of the job. Now, get ready."

Austin pushed Debare forward and then pulled him back.

"Before we enter, you'll need this." Austin handed him an earpiece that could barely fit in his hands. Debare put it in as they walked through the cooking staff's section.

Austin greeted a worker and Debare nodded. The man whispered to Austin something. That man then leads them to another room to change from their tuxedos into waiter outfits.

Austin instructed Debare to serve drinks to the Ministers at Table B and do it slowly to eavesdrop. Some waiters in the area looked at Debare suspiciously, but Austin told them in Russian Debare was in-training and that he was the regional manager. They laughed at a joke Austin made to break the ice.

"I can't serve Boris," said Debare before they went inside the ballroom.

"Why not?"

"He'll recognize me."

"Fine, serve Alina and her daughter and I'll serve the rest."

Austin opened the doors and high-class officials

were accompanied by their spouses. Everyone was laughing and talking. A pianist at a white grand set the mood. Austin pointed at a corner in the room; 'Table B' was lit up by a red mini lamp. Alina was alongside with her youngest daughter, Tatiana who resembled Gala and another man.

"Don't leave my sight," warned Austin as he disappeared into the crowd.

"Champagne for Table B?"

Alina and her attendants looked the Nigerian strangely. Tatiana was first to take a glass and then Alina and the man followed, thanking Debare.

"Get us some snacks, please," Alina suddenly ordered.

"Right away" Debare nodded whispering, "Fucking brat!"

The Nigerian headed to the kitchen grabbing the first snack tray he spotted. "Where the fuck is Austin?" Debare looked in the crowd but couldn't find him.

When Debare returned, Alina and Gala were there chatting while the third was in the lobby taking a phone call. Tatiana grabbed a few pieces of chocolate.

"Is that all, madam?"

"That's all unless you can dance for me."

"No, ma'am. I'm sorry but I cannot. I'm on duty." Debare turned away, mumbling, "What a fucking racist!"

Alina put her hand over her mouth but soon apologised. Debare nodded walking off while hearing a beep in his earpiece. It was Austin.

"Debare?"

"Where are you?" whispered Debare trying to spot him in the crowd.

"Go to the second floor now!"

Debare rushed upstairs. "Which door?"

"The last on the right."

————

Austin was kneeling next to a drunken man. "This is Vlad, my friend. He discovered the diamonds. Now, he will be fucking famous."

"Yes, that's me—your friend and mine," slurred Vlad.

Debare closed the door. "What about Alina downstairs?" whispered Debare.

"What's the fucking—big secret?" blurted Vlad.

"We're projecting your movie. You'll be a star in Hollywood," replied Austin.

Austin resumed his conversation with Debare. "Boris and Alina have nothing to do with the discovery. Let us find out more," Austin giggled while handing a glass of wine to Vlad.

"Now, Vlad. How did you get the diamonds? My

director here needs to know. Anything you tell us, we'll put it in your blockbuster."

"The owner of the Popigai Crater gave them to me. He knew I had the widest range of transportation--" His words slurred. "That fucking dirtbag owes me a lot of money, so let's call it payback." Vlad drank until the wine spilled down on his shirt.

Debare started recording their conversation, got closer and drank along with them.

"You're a rich man. Why do you need these diamonds, anyway?"

"They're for our people, not me; Russia's poor but many of my comrades are greedy."

"This news will make a good plot; A Russian who discovers diamonds to give them back to the poor," said Austin.

They laughed while Vlad pointed for Debare and Austin to drink more.

"Where are the other two?" asked Debare. Austin didn't want the Nigerian to interfere.

"Alina and Boris have them. I guess. Those two are some greedy motherfuckers. By the way, what does "motherfucker" mean?" slurred Vlad.

"I honestly don't know. Do you, Debare?"

Debare shrugged.

"Interesting! Vlad, you said Alina has a diamond, but Boris wants to sell the other," said Austin.

"I think Alina sold hers," interrupted Debare.

"Shut up?" interjected Austin.

"What the fuck did you say? Alina--" said Vlad.

"Let's talk about that part one more time. Give us a minute, Vlad. Help yourself."

Debare pulled Austin to a separate room. "MI6 gave me a tracker to put on her phone. She had the diamond weeks ago but its whereabouts have gone cold."

"What about Boris?"

"I don't know." Debare shrugged pondering over the diamond Nikita had on her neck.

Austin then returned and said, "We have more than enough to get your movie started."

But Vlad was passed out.

"Let's get out of here, Debare."

They exited and went back through the kitchen to their starting point.

"I have everything I need. You are free to go," said Austin.

"Wait, what are we going to do now?"

"Nothing. I'm going on vacation. Brian will call you. My job is finished." Austin lit up a cigarette and minutes later, the black van pulled up again.

"Nice working with you. You cocky bastard."

"Hey fuck some chicks while you're out here."

"Sir, yes, sir."

CHAPTER 7

Two weeks passed without much progress from MI6 and Debare was back at Nikita's. He crept inside her bedroom while she was in the shower. As Debare dug in her drawers, Nikita surprisingly came.

"What are you doing in here?" Nikita walked closer; she was covered in a towel and her head was still dripping wet.

"Organising your clothes. Man, your place is sloppy. I nearly tripped while coming in." The Nigerian closed the drawer before she noticed.

"My things are okay. You're not allowed in my personal space without permission. Remember, you're here to protect me, so go downstairs and stand by until I get ready." Just as Debare was leaving, Nikita's phone rang. She picked up as Debare reached the top of the steps.

"Boris, is our deal still on for tonight?"

"I don't know if I should bring the diamond. I almost got killed over it." Debare eavesdropped hoping to gather more. He leaned against the door hearing the words, "I miss you."

"This lady is just like her business," pondered Debare as Nikita kept talking.

Boris was married with young children. He looked like a piece of shit. "How could Nikita even fall for someone like that?" wondered Debare. As he tiptoed towards the steps, a vase flipped over from a mahogany stand.

"Wait, one second, sweetheart," said Nikita. Debare picked up the fragments and hurried down the steps. "Is that you, Matilda?"

Matilda, her housemaid, was downstairs and yelled back, "No." The old woman had the entire house smelling like pasta. Debare savored the smell and kept walking back and forth in the kitchen, looking inside. Matilda sensed his presence and offered him a small plate.

"Hmm, this almost tastes like Jollof."

The old woman smiled although it was clear she didn't understand English. Nikita came downstairs ten minutes later. Her hair was still wet, but she seemed mesmerized by the pasta.

"Debare, join me at the table, please."

"Tonight, I'm invited to a special engagement," spoke Nikita as Matilda set the table. "The venue will be packed with legislators, and I'll need you to guard me."

"What kind of special engagement, if you don't mind me asking?"

Nikita, while biting her food, presented the Nigerian a picture on her phone of a nude man. "It's an art expo celebrating Russian history."

"Anything else?"

"No, Debare."

"So, I guess there'll be a party afterward?"

"Yes, at Sky City."

———

Debare found out Nikita was meeting Boris at the Expo. He contacted Brian and his instructions were clear; gather intel only.

Nikita and Debare dined beforehand; gossiping away about life in Moscow and Nigeria. After an hour of Nikita getting dressed and some short fore-play, the two headed out. Debare drove, and neither of them spoke much while riding. Nikita sensed something.

"Is there something wrong, Peter?"

"No, why do you ask?"

"You're acting strange. May I shouldn't have played with you before we left?"

"No, it's okay. I'm just concentrating on tonight. That's all."

"I don't believe that. You sound like a jealous man."

"I'm not, Madame. We're almost there."

Minutes later, the Nigerian reached the Expo. He got out first, grabbing his earpiece and whispered, "Mic check." Brian responded, "All clear. Have fun!"

Nikita's dress was choking her in all the right places. Debare opened the car door for Nikita and watched her step out; fixing her dress and hair. As they went up hand in hand up the steps, the spotlight turned on her. The Expo was packed. "These ministers party so much, I wonder how they have time to help their people," pondered Debare.

"The diamond's in my handbag, Peter."

"Are you fucking crazy?" Debare grabbed her arm causing both to come to a stop.

"What is it now?

"We'll get killed over your foolishness?"

"That's why you're here, to protect me and you," Nikita said smiling.

"Alina!" Nikita yelled out excited, while Debare tried his best to conceal his face.

"Long time no see." Alina's voice was being picked up on the earpiece from afar.

"I missed you, how are the girls?"

"Oh, they're just lovely, we're sending off Daria to college this year."

Daria was the youngest of three siblings and the most polite.

"Send my hugs her way and tell her I wish her luck." Nikita hugged Alina goodbye.

Debare followed Nikita hoping Alina didn't recognize him. Boris was easy to spot. He and his wife were talking with a group of ministers. Nikita stopped.

"What's wrong?" asked Debare hearing Nikita curse Boris's wife under her breath.

"Hmm. Nothing."

Nikita then turned her attention to the exhibit's portraits. Throughout the night, Nikita was offered cocktails but Debare kindly refused anything sent her way.

After most began leaving, Boris saw Nikita telling her to meet him in the parking lot. Nikita told Debare to stay put but he didn't bother listening. He crept behind and hid behind a dumpster.

"The diamond, where is it, you stupid woman?" Boris screamed.

"I have it and why do you need it?"

"Excuse me? I need it, now. I don't have time for your childish games."

"Why? To give it to some other tramp?"

"Get your popcorn ready! Haha!," said Brian through the earpiece.

Boris slapped Nikita and the echo ricocheted through the parking lot. "How dare you, you fucking slut?"

She grabbed him. "You told me you would fucking divorce her! I believed you." Nikita began crying.

"Divorce my wife? For you, the head of the biggest prostitution ring in Moscow? Please." Boris laughed. "I would never divorce her for a low—life like you. But you know what we can do tomorrow morning on my way to work." Boris got close whispering something in her ear. Nikita pushed him away.

"You'll never get the diamond, you stupid bastard! I fucking hate you." Nikita slapped Boris and kicked him in the balls. Nikita then ran out the parking lot, crying. Debare couldn't stop laughing as Brian was ridiculing Nikita inside his earpiece. The Nigerian got back in time as Nikita neared him.

She was visibly agitated, wiping her tears. She told Debare to bring the car. When the Nigerian asked why she wasn't going to the afterparty, Nikita said she was tired.

———

The drive home was quiet, and Nikita told Debare to

take the car to his place for the night after letting her out.

Debare went home and when he arrived, he found the gate unlocked. Clutching his pistol, he crept inside. There were noises coming from the living room as he tiptoed. Brian saw his shadow and told him to put the gun down.

"You scared the shit out of me!" said Debare.

Austin was with him, watching TV and sipping on a beer.

"Why the fuck both of you are here anyway?"

"I have a spare key. Sometimes, I can't stay at home. My fucking girlfriend is getting on my nerves. These Russian girls just want to go out and party!" said Brian as Austin laughed.

"Anyway," replied Debare.

"I see you've been out working or working out?"

"Running errands, you mean."

"In a tux?"

"Art Expo. You heard the shit."

"Enough of the small talk. We need to debrief," said Brian.

"Ok, give me a minute to change."

———

Austin began speaking. "The fourth diamond is still missing."

"It's still missing? Shit! We don't have any intel on its location?" added Brian.

"No, we have to go over the clues we have so far," Austin sat up. "Alina sold hers and got two billion dollars. She's the richest fucking woman in Russia."

"There's nothing we can do now but I got a feeling that the last is with that dirtbag, Boris. He's the most dangerous; working for the Russian Mafia part-time."

"Part-time? Debare chuckled. "I've been on Nikita, but can't get close enough to verify if she has a real or fake one," added Debare.

"Let's assume it's real for now. Now back to Boris, MI6 found he's taking a business trip this weekend," added Austin.

"A business trip? Maybe he's going to sell the remaining diamond? With the Parliament's sessions wrapped up, it's the perfect cover," said Brian excitedly.

"Hey, Brian. My trails on Alina got cold and I need to get back to her before we lose her," suggested Austin.

Brian looked at Debare having second thoughts if the Nigerian should be the one trailing Boris. "I guess you have another job, kiddo."

———

"We'll be late, hurry!" Nikita rushed out, tossing Debare her luggage. They are traveling to Novorossiysk, 1,500 kilometres from Moscow. Boris invited Nikita on the business trip and Debare sensed it was a trap. The Nigerian started growing a beard and looked aged. From Boris' conversations before the trip, intel suggested he was going to get the diamond from Nikita, one way or the other.

After the flight, Debare and Nikita were driven to an exotic hotel called the Expromt, paid for by Boris. Nikita's suite was huge, and she raved about it. Before they coming downstairs, Debare and Nikita made out.

"Don't be upset if you see something between Boris and me, Peter. It's only business." She grabbed Debare's cock while the elevator descended. "I'll take care of this big ole thing later when I get back." She kissed Debare causing him to moan.

"No--No worries, Madam. I--I'm at your service," slurred the Nigerian.

The elevator doors opened to a ball in the lobby's terrace. Debare was close to her, looking serious as Nikita walked in. Everyone complimented her for her fancy attire.

"So where is he?" asked Debare.

Nikita looked around for Boris. "Let's get a drink." Minutes later, Boris arrived with his personal bodyguard. His eyes were fixed on Nikita and stepped right over.

"I see you finally made it."

"I wouldn't miss it for the world." Nikita smiled as Boris eyed her sexy figure. He kissed her on the cheek and then looked at Debare. "You are?"

"Peter, sir." Debare put his hand for Boris to shake.

"I see you found yourself a job." Boris mocked as Nikita appeared confused.

"Do you two know each other?"

"We met a few weeks ago at the refugee protest. You were the one who gave me my pen back. Right?"

"Yes, sir. It was me. Madame Nikita has been very gracious in giving me this job, sir."

"Enough of the small talk, let's have a good time. Nice seeing you again, Peter." Boris walked off with Nikita.

They spoke in a corner as Debare stood by Boris' bodyguard catching Nikita's chat through the earpiece.

"We are waiting for Grigor to come. He'll have the money," said Boris. Nikita was excited and it appears she was selling the diamond.

———

As nightfall descended, the reception area was congested, Debare got word that he had to stop the diamond from being sold. Boris and Nikita dipped out for an hour and Debare knew they were fucking. Once they returned, they came back to the gala briefly and then headed to the elevators. Debare put down his drink and followed them, dodging behind the wall corner. He tried getting closer as overheard they were getting ready to meet with Grigor.

"He's almost here," said Boris after closing his flip phone.

"Debare! Debare!" yelled Brian in his earpiece.

"Shut up!" Debare pulled the earpiece out.

Boris and Nikita were still at the elevator when Debare ran into them. Nikita turned around happy to see the Nigerian.

"Peter, come here."

"Yes, Madam?"

"You'll escort a man inside by the name of Grigor when he arrives. We'll be in Room 340." Nikita winked as they walked inside the elevator.

Debare nodded and went back to the lobby.

"I'm taking my break now," shouted the receptionist to the doorman.

"Ok," shouted the doorman back leaving him to do desk duty. Grigor arrived, standing outside the parking lot,. He was talking on his cellphone while smoking a cigarette.

"Think fast, Debare," whispered Debare to

himself. Debare looked around spotting no one. He went back to the elevator and then crept back to the desk. Once the Nigerian was behind him, he injected him with a syringe causing the doorman to fall to the ground asleep. He was snoring like a baby within seconds.

Debare carried him to a nearby closet and removed his hat and his nametag. The Nigerian came out to the front desk fixing himself as Grigor walked through the sliding doors looking around. He was wearing a tailor-made Italian suit.

"Good evening sir, may I help you with your luggage?"

Grigor smiled. "Oh, pardon me. I haven't used English for a long time. But thank you, I have nothing but a carryon," said Grigor looking towards the elevators.

"Have you checked-in online?"

"No, but I'm here to visit a few of my colleagues from work. Perhaps you can assist me?"

"The names, please." Debare moved away from the desk trying to hurry just in case the receptionist came back.

"Boris Petrov and Nikita Andreeva."

Debare looked noticing that Grigor wasn't alone. Four men in black leather jackets were standing outside, wearing sunglasses, looking around. Debare knew the men were after Grigor.

Debare motioned for Grigor to follow him to the elevator. The men in black came inside to the reception as the receptionist came back to greet them.

"How can I help you gentlemen this evening?" she said in Russian.

"Out of our way, you fucking bitch," one man pushed her on the ground as they ran to the elevators.

Debare and Grigor hurried inside and the doors closed. They heard the men loud voices and banging on the door as the elevator ascended.

"What's going on? Those men? Where are we going?

Debare told him he was taking him to Nikita and Boris. The elevator reached the last floor, and they got off. Luckily, there was only one elevator working.

"Where are Boris and Nikita?"

"Just down the hall, we're almost there." He pushed Grigor in front of him.

Debare grabbed his pistol and hit Grigor in the back of the head, causing him to faint. Then, he dragged him to a nearby closet. Moments later, Nikita called the Nigerian. "What's taking so fucking long?" she said screaming.

"Grigor's not here yet. I'm in the lobby," said Debare going to the maintenance lift on the other side.

"Check outside, maybe he's lost. Hurry up!"

"Okay. The connection is cutting out—." Debare hung up and pressed the down button. The doors suddenly opened and four men walked off, grabbing Debare.

"What do you think you're doing?" Debare tried fighting them off. The men said nothing as they blindfolded him and took him away.

———

The blindfold was removed and the men stood over the Nigerian wearing black masks. "Where the fuck am I?" Debare was seated while the men were looking at him.

"What the hell is going on here?"

"Shut the fuck up." Debare was slapped in the back of the head causing him to jerk.

Another person came in. He pulled off his mask and revealed his face.

"Brian!?" said Debare.

"How dare you, you fucking bloody traitor!" Brian's face was red as he slapped Debare across his face making his head jerk again. "How could you do this to me!? I trusted you for God's sake!"

"What did I do? What the hell, Brian?"

"What did you do, huh? You've been hiding intel."

"What are you talking about? I told you Nikita has a diamond and I don't know if it's real."

"You want it for yourself. Don't you?" Brian crossed his arms.

"No, I don't. I was trying to do the mission myself to show you I'm worthy."

Brian hiring Austin to replace him made Debare expendable. The Nigerian feared going to prison for life.

"You did nothing, fucking nothing!" said Brian tossing the books on the table. "If you wanted to tell us the truth, you would've done it from the beginning. You despicable piece of shit. Did you think I wouldn't find out, stupid fuck? You can't hide anything from me." Debare hoped the earth would open and swallow him first before hearing Brian's taunts.

"Is Boris with her?"

Debare didn't answer thinking if he told Brian that they would kill Nikita.

"Boris is smarter than we think. They probably already left," said Brian prancing the room with three other agents.

"Answer me, you fucking prick!" Brian punched Debare in the face.

"Yes, yes."

"What fucking room?"

"Room 340."

"What are you waiting for? Go now!" Brian ordered his men and turned back to Debare. "I swear I'll make your life a living hell from now on. I have the fucking power to wipe you off the face of this Earth with a snap of my finger. You hear me?" Brian turned away from Debare and took a phone call from central command. Debare didn't move; shocked.

"How long has the affair been going on between Nikita and Boris?"

"I don't know."

"Her fucking boy-toy bodyguard doesn't know? Get the fuck out of here!"

"I don't know honestly."

"Spare me your ignorance, please."

"They are a thing, that's all I know."

Brian didn't reply back looking at Debare's face, disgusted.

Ten minutes passed since Brian's men left. The group stormed in, panicking.

"Sir, there's no one there." said the leader. Brian turned to Debare, "Where are they heading or I will kill you right now?"

"I don't know. They were meeting Grigor. That's all I know."

"Search the fucking hotel from top to bottom." "As for you, you will find Nikita and that diamond, you clumsy fuck."

CHAPTER 8

The saga with Brian appeared to have no end. Now, Brian's agents were in and out of Debare's flat monitoring him and any communications on the feeds. There was an awkward silence while the agents were working and Debare was told to stay away. Meanwhile, MI6 had no clue on where Boris and Nikita had gone.

The Nigerian frustrated with Brian's orders broke his phone. Three days later, he received another by DHL. Brian told him if he had one more fuckup, he would be sent back to Nigeria. When the Nigerian put his Sim card in, a message popped up from Nikita.

"You disappeared out of nowhere, sweetheart. I'm home but not staying long. I'll see you soon – Nikita."

Brian came a few minutes later. "Hey, I heard you received a package? Where is it?"

Debare was clutching the phone in his hand and

Brian took it from him. "What do we have here?" Brian's smile faded as he read the message.

"She's in Moscow? Quick, get to her house now!" Brian rushed Debare pushing him towards the door. The agents got up as well logging out their laptops. "Check her fucking house up and down. "Take this tracker with you. Don't fuck this up, boy."

Brian didn't trust Debare to go by himself, so he sent Austin to trail him. Austin was waiting out front and they drove to Nikita's. The gate was locked, and the keypad was shut off. Matilda heard knocking on the door and came. When she saw Debare, she waved. She let the Nigerian and Austin inside and showed them to the living room.

"Nikita was here two hours ago. I don't know why she left suddenly," said Matilda saddened. Austin translated and tried comforting her. "It's fine, I'm sure she'll come back soon." Austin said in Russian nudging Debare to go on and speak.

"Listen, Matilda, Nikita forgot something and told me to take it from her room if that's not a problem." The Nigerian caressed her shoulder and the old woman smiled. "Go ahead, but please don't make a mess, Peter."

The room was straighten up apart from Nikita's closet. Her outfits were tossed everywhere, and the safe was left open.

"Fuck," snapped Austin. "Brian's going to kill us."

Debare told him to check every drawer whilst he checked under the mattress. Austin pulled out boxes of jewellery, but there was nothing but cheap gold necklaces inside. "The diamond's gone." Austin stopped, placing his hands on top of his head.

"What do we do now?" Austin told Debare to stop searching for the moment.

"Think Debare! Think! Where could have she hid it?"

"She never let me even come close to that thing. I know we need to hurry!"

They went downstairs, seeing Matilda cleaning the living room. "Matilda, did Nikita leave anything for me?"

"Oh yes, I forgot. There's an envelope. I don't know what's inside."

"Can you bring it?"

"It's in her office on the table down the hall."

Debare led the way while Austin stormed inside. The envelope was there and Austin grabbed it and tried ripping it open. Debare snatched it away. "It's mine." The Nigerian pulled out a stack of American hundred dollar bills, with a note saying: "Sorry, I wasn't able to pay you for your services. Perhaps we'll meet again."

"Nikita's gone forever," said Debare.

"Matilda!" Austin yelled. Matilda ran to the room stopping at the door with the duster in her hand. "Yes!"

"Do you have any idea where Nikita might've gone?"

"I don't know. That girl goes anywhere her feet will carry her."

"Just anything," pleaded Austin.

"I've known Nikita since she was a little girl. She was never like this until she became--." Matilda sat down holding her head.

"She's like my little girl. Her parents were always away and I was the one who basically took care of her." Matilda stated wiping away her tears.

Austin continued asking questions, but Matilda didn't want to say anything that would jeopardise Nikita's life. "Matilda, thank you for your time. I think we need to get going." Austin pulled on Debare.

As they were leaving, Debare's phone buzzed. A text message came in from Brian: "Go to the Parliament now, Alina's being arrested."

Debare showed it to Austin and he said: "Let's go!"

———

"I wonder why the police are arresting her," said Debare while Austin was driving.

"While you were busy attending to Nikita's

fancies, Brian pulled a fast one." Once they arrived, Debare jumped out first. The street was swarmed with news vans and many people on the scene.

"Stop! You have no right to do this!" yelled Alina as she was being taken away, handcuffed.

Police and military personnel were in front of the Parliament building guarding as the other Ministers watched in shock. Debare looked over at Austin who was chuckling.

"What now?" asked Debare.

"We must find Nikita and Boris."

Alina's attorneys took a position to answer questions about allegations. Shortly after it was over, Austin and Debare left. There was an unmarked car parked in the front. Debare opened the door finding Brian seated and another man standing above him.

"Brian?"

The man turned around. It was Vlad, the lead behind the Cullinan search.

"You must be Debare?" Vlad stood up to shake the Nigerian's hand.

"Yes, sir." Debare dodged looking at him.

Vlad was wearing a fancy suit and had an expensive-looking suitcase beside the couch.

"I heard a lot about you, son."

"Oh, yeah! I hope good things." Debare looked over to Brian.

"I'm Austin, sir," said Austin butting in. Vlad shook his hand and then sat. "Gentleman, we have work to do. Please sit down."

"Sadly, we have no new leads on the whereabouts of Nikita and Boris." Brian looked disgusted.

"They've probably have left Russia by now, but our intelligence is not 100% certain." Vlad began digging through his suitcase. "Let's not assume they haven't. I believe we need to break up our operations in search parties."

Debare wasn't paying attention and Brian kicked his leg under the table. Vlad chuckled knowing. "We'll find them. Everyone knows their profiles. Interpol has been alerted and we need the CCTV coverage at the borders for the last 24 hours." Vlad's laptop was being powered on as he spoke.

"That wouldn't be an issue. We have access to them," interrupted Brian.

"I don't think they left Russia yet. Austin and I just spoke to her maid, Matilda who said she was at the house a few hours ago," claimed Debare.

"Maybe she was lying," interrupted Austin.

"I planted a tracker on Boris' bag on my first assignment. If it's still working, maybe we can track him," replied Debare.

"I doubt he'd carry that bag around. Someone

would probably easily recognise him," said Vlad. "Sometimes, we find the trackers on dogs and cats."

Everyone laughed especially Debare who was the loudest.

"Seriously, knock it off. We can't sure, anyway. Let's break up this party and start with the CCTVs," commanded Vlad.

"I'll coordinate my men in the eastern region to begin accessing them," said Austin.

"I'll telelink the feeds through our cables back in the UK," added Brian.

"Tonight, we'll regroup. Time's not on our side, gentlemen. Let's go."

Vlad grabbed his laptop and other equipment and left while Austin went in a different direction. Debare was instructed to keep tabs on Nikita's house. He took the Metro to stay close in hopes she'd come back. The Nigerian went to a nearby cafe which was filled with cigarette and cigar smoke. It was almost impossible for Debare to find a spot to set up in peace.

While browsing through his phone, it rang. The call was from an unknown number.

"Hello?"

"It's me, Matilda. Meet me at the Red Square in 20 minutes."

"You speak English—?" Before his sentence ended, the phone hung up.

Debare looked up the location and saw he wasn't far from Red Square.

———

"Next stop: Red Square."

People were there taking snapshots and admiring the spectacle. There were many tourists, mainly from China. Debare waited in the cold, blowing his hands hoping Matilda would come quickly.

Minutes later, the old woman came up from behind the Nigerian. "Come, let's sit down somewhere." Debare walked behind her to a nearby coffee shop inside a plaza. Matilda ordered a cup of tea and Debare declined.

"I don't trust that Austin boy, so I need this to tell you alone. Nikita's still in Moscow."

"Where?"

The waiter came and Matilda paid him.

"I'm not sure, but I think she's at one of her old flats that are up for sale," said Matilda sipping.

"Do you know where?"

"I have a few mailing addresses, but I'm not sure if they are actually the places. She never told me where."

"You've been a great help. I'm trying to stop her from getting killed. These men are dangerous. Do you know if Boris is still with her?"

"I believe so. Yesterday, his wife called our house screaming. The crazy woman found out about him and Nikita."

"Why is Nikita so in love with that ugly guy anyway?"

"She's never been in love. Her father was never around when she was younger. He was always working abroad. When Boris met Nikita, she viewed him as a father figure. He took advantage of her childishness and she fell for his charm. You know what I'm saying?"

Debare laughed. "I know exactly what you are saying."

"Nikita and Boris met about years ago. I remember when he first came to the house. They carried in bottles of expensive wine every time he visited and spent a few nights a week together." Matilda looked down at one spot as she spoke. "It was the first time I ever saw my little Nikita smile so much." Matilda's hands then began shaking. "Now, she runs off with this crazy man. I never like him personally. Nikita gave her heart to this ugly ass motherfucker."

They laughed and Debare held her hands.

———

Matilda excused herself. Debare hugged her and promised he'd find and protect Nikita. The Nigerian looked at the mailing addresses and hurried out to begin searching. Debare had a few hours left before meeting back with Brian, Austin, and Vlad at his flat.

The Metro ride was short and the Nigerian checked the first mailing address on his GPS. Debare pondered why Nikita would buy property in such a ravaged neighbourhood.

Once he reached the place, he headed up to the seventh floor. The building appeared to only have a few tenants. "Apartment 57." He pulled out a set of tweezers and had picked the lock.

The place was small and Nikita was nowhere to be found. The Nigerian closed the door and went back to the Metro. The second location was only three blocks from the station in a better area. There were wealthy people residing there and it would be harder to get in. After the Nigerian told the security guard of his relationship with Nikita, he let him in. But, she wasn't there either.

It was almost nine at night, and Debare was smoking inside the parking lot of his home. When he opened his door, Vlad, Austin, and Brian were already inside.

"Did you come up with anything?" asked Brian.

"Matilda gave me addresses of two apartments, but Nikita wasn't there."

"We'll never find them!" Vlad said angrily. He stood up and walked over to the balcony.

"We didn't find anything on the CCTVs, so they must still be in the country," said Austin.

Austin turned on the TV and saw something. "Hey shut up."

"Please return our father to us! We'll pay anything!" said Boris' daughters assuming someone kidnapped their father.

"What the fuck is this?" yelled Brian.

"Sounds like the world believes someone kidnapped Boris," said Vlad not surprised. The news conference ended with a commercial break.

"Debare, quick give me the IP address of Boris' tracker," commanded Brian. Debare took out his phone and kept scrolling through the codes. He gave it to Brian who gave it to Vlad. For minutes, the room was in suspense as Vlad kept punching keys on his laptop.

"Gentleman, we have a fucking location."

"Yes!" shouted Debare, pumping his fist in the air.

CHAPTER 9

"We're going to St. Petersburg, fellas, so bundle up. It's colder than a motherfucker out there. Meet back in thirty," Vlad ordered Brian, Austin, and Debare and a small contingent of agents.

Within an hour, everyone was onboard Vlad's black van heading through a bad snowstorm for a 9-hour drive to St. Petersburg. Brian was given instructions to do whatever to get the diamond even if it costed lives. The team's weapons were locked and loaded. Boris was identified as target #1 and Nikita #2. No one knew how this will end. Thoughts raced through Debare's mind as they were given preparations from Vlad and Brian.

The snowstorm was so awful that flights in and out of Moscow had been cancelled. Vlad in the meantime hacked Nikita's IWatch after discovering the tracking device in Boris's suitcase suddenly stopped sending signals.

"Apartment 10B. Dernov Apartment House. I've got them." screamed Vlad. "Maybe Nikita is making love with the watch on. There's a bunch of movements."

Everybody laughed.

The overall plan was for the Nigerian to first persuade Nikita to surrender before the Russian forces got to them and executed them in cold blood.

Brian warned Debare that if he fucked up, he wouldn't hesitate to execute Debare himself and the mission would be ended. Debare laughed at Brian, but Brian was serious.

"How far away are we?" asked Austin, seated next to the driver.

"About fifteen minutes away, sir."

Brian continued looking out the window while talking on the satellite phone with Robert, the division chief of MI6 in London. Brian kept reassuring him the mission would be a success.

The countrymen as they drove by appeared to live in simplicity while the marketplaces were crowded with merchants and farm animals. The scenery reminded Debare of markets back home. After this experience, he promised himself to never cheat a customer ever again.

The black van made a sharp turn and then stopped on an empty street a few blocks away from St. Petersburg's central market.

"This is your stop, Debare. Check your earpiece to see if it's on. Pay attention to every detail we've gone over and don't mess up." Brian patted him on the back.

Debare gave the team a thumbs up. This was his sovereign chance, and the Nigerian knew it.

———

The van pulled off, and they left the operation in Debare's hands. The unit went on standby as each team member exited a few blocks apart, disguised as locals strolling. Debare walked until he reached the parking area of an 18th-century Victorian building. A security guard met Debare with his hand on his old gun. "How can I help you?" the guard responded in English seeing Debare. The man's old wrinkly face showed he'd been working this same job for most of his life.

"I forgot my keys inside the condo. I just moved in yesterday," chuckled Debare. The guard wasn't amused.

"I don't remember seeing your face around here. When did you move in?"

"The other guard - he was fat - came to help me up with my stuff two nights ago."

"Oleg's helping someone out? That's a first." The old man laughed and told Debare to come inside.

The Nigerian shook his hand and took the stairs. He readied himself as he came closer to the suite. Making his eyes watery, the Nigerian tapped on the door of Apartment 10B. Waiting for what seemed like ages, Nikita opened the door wearing a sheer bodysuit.

"Nikita! Oh, Baby! I missed you." Debare's tears dropped as he embraced her. Nikita's hair was cut short and dyed brown.

"Peter?" said Nikita looking puzzled.

"Do you know how hard it was to find you, my love?"

"Come inside. I was just cleaning up." Nikita led him to the living room.

"Where were you? God, you'll get yourself killed. I got the envelope from Matilda," said Debare taking a seat.

"I've been busy with my businesses. I needed a break away from home." Nikita sat across from Debare. Vlad was trying to get through the Nigerian's earpiece but there was static.

"What the fuck? Not now," murmured Debare.

"Debare, can you hear me? The men are almost

near your location. Keep her busy." Vlad's voice kept interrupting Debare's attention.

"Nice." Debare slurred his words; partly responding to Nikita but signalling to Vlad, okay.

"So, how did you find me?"

"Matilda told me to help you get out of this mess. She gave me a few addresses but still, I couldn't find you. There was a broadcast on TV claiming that Boris had been kidnapped."

Nikita looked at Debare unconvinced.

"Matilda, of course." Nikita gazed at her nails.

"She cares for you, Nikita and I do, too. I'm grateful for this job and I take it seriously."

"I see. So, she told you one of my secrets. How's she doing?" Nikita changed her facial expression.

"She's okay but sad because you're not around. She calls you her little girl."

"I am that for sure."

"Debare! Debare! Are you there? The connection's kept giving static. Is Nikita with you? We're waiting for you," said Brian.

"Now, Peter. You must be thirsty. I see you're sweating. Care for a drink?" She got up waiting not waiting for Debare to reply.

"Sure and fuck the shit out of her while we come there. We're minutes away," joked Vlad in the earpiece. "Tell her you to need to go to the bathroom and run the sink. Our thermal indicators have spotted the diamond inside the safe. Get to her room. I'm working on hacking it open for you right now!"

Debare was about to get up when Nikita came out of the kitchen with two glasses. "Here you go, my love." She stared at him. Debare took the glass and took a small sip. She came next to him and put her legs on top of his. Debare pushed her away gently.

"What's wrong, baby?"

"Nothing. I have to use the bathroom."

"Ok, take another sip first before you leave me. This is the best wine Russia has to offer. I'll take care of that big black thing when you come back."

Her words began slurring in Debare's mind as he took a few more sips. She lifted her glass in unison as the Nigerian went down the hallway. Debare noticed her room was next to the bathroom. He turned on the water and gathered himself. A minute later, he crept out into Nikita's room and forgot to close the bathroom door. There was a big trunk on top of her drawers. He opened it, going through everything inside; finding only necklaces and rings. Debare then got on his knees passing through each drawer but there was no diamond.

"Debare, are you inside? We are having a hard time getting in. The guard isn't at his post. Do you copy?" said Brian through the earpiece.

"Maybe he's on break. Hurry the fuck up! I don't see a safe here," whispered Debare.

As the Nigerian stood up, he noticed someone in the mirror. It was Nikita holding the Cullinan diamond in one hand and a gun in the other. "Looking for this?"

He turned around slowly facing her. "Yes, actually but it's not what you see."

"Save it, you treacherous fool! You're a bad man. I've trusted you and twice you have betrayed me. Guess what—" Nikita's words began slurring again and Debare's eyesight started blearing. Quickly, he was losing his senses and began kneeling.

"What have you done? I'm here to save you. You don't understand."

"Did you think you and your agents were going to get my diamond?"

The Nigerian felt a sharp pain in his heart and realised Nikita had poisoned him.

"Call a fucking ambulance. I don't want to die. I have a mother who needs me."

"Don't we all, Peter? I gave you something that would put you to sleep for a little while."

Debare's heart rate was irregular; slowing down as blood rushed to his brain. "Brian, come now, please! She poisoned me," said Debare.

"We're inside, kiddo. We're coming!" yelled Brian in the earpiece.

"May we see each other again--in the next life," said Nikita staring at Debare's pale face. She bent over and kissed his forehead as Debare's heart had stopped.

His body laid lifeless on the floor. Nikita went to pick up the earpiece which fell out Debare's ear. "You killed this good man, you fucking Americans."

"You fucking bitch. I will—" replied Brian.

Nikita stomped the earpiece to pieces and quickly gathered her things and left.

"Debare, Debare!" yelled Brian and Vlad. "Abort mission. Abort mission," yelled Brian and Vlad to the agents in their earpieces. They were already inside as they were making their way upstairs.

———

Nikita's obsession with the Cullinan diamond was more than her love for her own self. Its beauty mesmerised her and she'd do anything to protect it. She received intel from the Kremlin hours earlier and killed Boris by electrocuting him in her bathtub minutes before Debare arrived. Debare didn't see the body which was behind the shower curtains.

As the sole owner of the last Cullinan diamond,

Nikita became Russia's most powerful woman. She never wed and returned to her maid, Matilda who asked her about Peter's whereabouts. Nikita replied that he'd gone back to Nigeria because his mother was ill. Matilda knew she was lying but remained loyal until her death only a week later. Nikita had to tie up loose ends and Matilda's treasonable offense made her expendable.

Two weeks passed since Debare's death and his family in Nigeria kept coming to the shop asking Daraja about his whereabouts. She said told them he was away in China growing the business. It was a lie Brian told her when he paid the rent and her salary every month. As long as her money was there, Daraja didn't ask any questions.

Vlad stayed behind in Russia while Austin and Brian went back to the UK. The BBC later interviewed MI6 after a WikiLeaks revelation tied them to the Nigerian's death. MI6 denied the allegations and said it was fake news.

Although they publicly denied the report, MI6 regularly remembered Debare as the Nigerian who lost his life. Brian and Austin spoke of him often as they drank after work, always tipping their glasses to the Nigerian who gave his life for the cost of his freedom.